The Rock in the Road

by Jill Brasell
illustrated by Peter Campbell

Learning Media

Characters

RABBIT
DOG
HORSE
GOAT
MOUSE

For this play, try using a cushion for the rock and a chair for the wheelbarrow.

RABBIT *is walking down the road pushing a wheelbarrow. A big rock is in the way.*

2

RABBIT. Bother! I'll never get past this rock. I'll have to push it out of the way.

    RABBIT tries to push the rock, but it won't move. **DOG** *comes along.*

DOG. What's the matter, Rabbit?

RABBIT. There's a rock in the way and I can't get past. I've tried to move it, but it just won't budge.

3

DOG. Let me try to pull it out of the way.

    DOG *tries to pull the rock, but it won't move.*

DOG. No. I can't move it one little bit.
How can we get past?

    DOG *sits down with* **RABBIT.** **GOAT** *comes along.*

GOAT. Why are you two sitting here?

DOG. We can't get past this rock.

RABBIT. I tried to push it out of the way.

DOG. And I tried to pull it out of the way.

RABBIT *and* **DOG.** But it just won't budge!

GOAT. Let me try to push it out of the way. Goats are very good at pushing. **GOAT** *pushes the rock, but it doesn't move.*

GOAT. You're right. It's too heavy. We can't get past.

*GOAT sits down with **RABBIT** and **DOG**. **HORSE** comes along.*

HORSE. What's the matter with you three?

RABBIT. We can't get past this rock. I tried to push it.

GOAT. So did I!

DOG. And I tried to pull it out of the way.

RABBIT, GOAT, *and* **DOG.** But it just won't budge!

HORSE. Let me try. Horses are very good at pulling.

*They throw a rope over the rock and **HORSE** pulls.*

HORSE. You're right. It's too heavy. We can't get past.

HORSE *sits down with* **RABBIT, DOG,** *and*
GOAT. MOUSE *comes along.*

MOUSE. What are you four doing?

RABBIT. We can't get past this rock. I
tried to push it.

GOAT. So did I!

DOG. I tried to pull it.

HORSE. So did I!

RABBIT, GOAT, DOG, *and* **HORSE.** But it just
won't budge!

9

MOUSE. I know how to move this rock.

RABBIT *(laughing)*. You! How could a little mouse move such a big rock? It's too big for a rabbit to move.

DOG. And it's too big for a dog to move.

GOAT. It's too big for a goat to move.

HORSE. And it's too big for a horse to move.

MOUSE. Yes. But it's not too big for a rabbit, a dog, a goat, a horse, and a mouse to move … together!

RABBIT, DOG, GOAT, *and* **HORSE.** Yes! That's what we can do!

All of the animals push against the rock, and it slowly moves out of the way.

EVERYONE. Hooray!

Now we can all get past.